Jamie.
So you want to be a dog?

W9-BYF-878

Osage

LFL

So You Want to Be a Dog?

Adaptation by Jamie White

Based on TV series teleplays

written by Raye Lankford and Peter K. Hirsch

Based on characters created by Susan Meddaugh

HOUGHTON MIFFLIN HARCOURT

Boston • New York • 2013

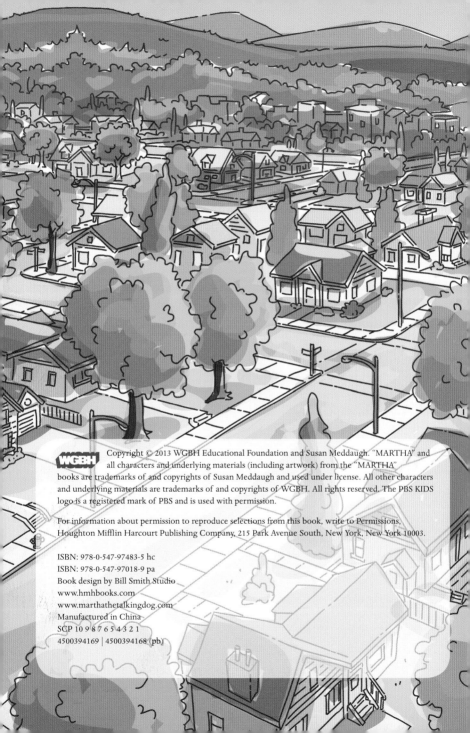

For information about permission to reproduce selections from this book, write to Permissions,
Houghton Mifflin Harcourt Publishing Company, 215 Park Avenue South, New York, New York 10003.

ISBN: 978-0-547-97483-5 hc
ISBN: 978-0-547-97018-9 pa
Book design by Bill Smith Studio
www.hmhbooks.com
www.marthathetalkingdog.com
Manufactured in China
SCP 10 9 8 7 6 5 4 3 2 1
4500394169 | 4500394168 (pb)

MARTHA SAYS HELLO

So you want to be a dog? Hey, who doesn't? But before you start hanging out at hydrants or barking at your friends, read this book to see what a dog's life is *really* like. You might be surprised to learn that it can be a little *ruff*. Take it from me, Martha!

Of course, I'm not exactly your common canine. Ever since Helen fed me her alphabet soup, I've been able to speak. And speak and speak . . . No one's sure how or why, but the letters in the soup traveled up to my brain instead of down to my stomach.

Now as long as I eat my daily bowl of alphabet soup, I can talk. To my family—Helen, baby Jake, Mom, Dad, and Skits, who only speaks Dog. To Helen's best human friend, T.D. To anyone who'll listen.

Sometimes my family wishes I didn't talk quite so much. But living with a talking dog has its perks. Like the time I entered a contest on the radio and won us a weekend at the Come-On-Inn!

And if I couldn't talk, I wouldn't be able to tell you this story. It's about what happened when two of my human friends became dogs for a day. Have *you* ever wanted to be a dog? Then you'd better read on . . .

DOG DAY AFTERNOON

Story #1

If you're going to be a dog, then you'll want a good human. Helen is my human. We have lots of fun together. But when she hurt her ankle, all she could do was lie on the couch.

"Why don't you lick it?" I asked. "That's what I do when my paw hurts."

"I can't lick my ankle," said Helen.

"Want me to lick it?" I offered.

Helen scratched my head.

"You're sweet, but—"

She was interrupted by the arrival of her cousin, Carolina. "Hey, lazybones!" Carolina teased. "What are you doing on the couch?"

"I sprained my ankle in gym class," Helen replied.

"Oh, I can totally empathize," said Carolina. "I once sprained my ankle running to the mall. My foot looked like an eggplant for a week, but I got the cutest shorts for half off."

"Mmm! What's in there?" I asked, sniffing the paper bag in her hand.

Carolina held it away from me. "Tamales. For *humans*."

Figures.

"My dad made them for our sleepover," she said, heading into the kitchen. She set her bag on the counter, where she saw a piece of paper. "Helen, did you see this note?"

"What's it say?" Helen called.

" 'Remember to take Martha to the vet,' "
read Carolina.

"Uh, that's trash," I said.

Helen sat up. "I completely forgot! Martha
has to go in for her shots."

"Don't be a hero, Helen!"
I pleaded. "Lie back down. The vet can wait till
you get better. Longer, even. Actually, forever!"

"Martha's right," said Carolina. "You shouldn't
put pressure on that ankle."

"Listen to Carolina," I said. "She knows what
she's talking about."

"I'll take Martha to the vet," Carolina offered.

"Don't listen to *her!*" I cried. "She doesn't know what she's talking about!"

But it was too late. "Come on, Martha," said Carolina. "I'll get the leash."

LEASH?! This day is getting worse by the minute, I thought. Dog Rule #15: At the first sight of a leash, RUN!

I bolted out the door.

"Martha, come here!" Carolina shouted, chasing me down the sidewalk. "I need you on the leash!"

I stopped. "Why?"

"So you don't run off."

"*Me? Run off?*"

But then I heard a *chitter-chatter* behind me. "SQUIRREL!" I shouted, running after it. Oh, yeah. There's nothing like chasing

a squirrel up a tree to make a dog forget her troubles.

"Martha, get over here!" Carolina ordered.

And I would have. Honest. If I hadn't smelled . . . "MEAT!" I cried, taking off again. I tracked the scent to a trash can, found a sandwich, and swallowed it in one gulp. "Mmm. Bologna!"

Carolina caught up with me. "Come here *NOW!*"

"All right, all right. I will in— Whoa, MUD!" I splashed into a gloopy puddle.

Ahhh! Mud, meat, and squirrels. What more could a dog ask for? This day had really turned around. Until a hand clipped the leash onto my collar.

"Gotcha!" said Carolina.

I DON'T LIKE GOING TO THE VET

I don't like wearing a leash. I don't like going to the vet. I DON'T like wearing a leash to the vet. So why was Carolina the one moaning?

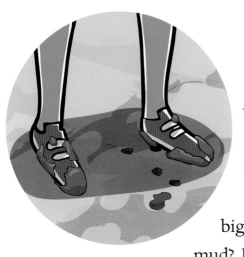

"Shoes! Mud!" she wailed, frowning at her feet. "MUD SHOES!"

What was the big woof about a little mud? I had just rolled my whole body in mud. It was delightful.

Carolina's mud shoes went *squelch, squelch* all the way to the vet's office. Even though it was my appointment, she lay on the doctor's table and winced.

The vet cleaned the mud off Carolina's shoes. "There," she said. "All done."

"Thanks, doc," I said, creeping toward the exit. "Send us a bill."

"Not yet," she said. "It's time for your shot."

She set me on the table and took out a long needle.

"I was afraid you'd say that," I said. "It's tough being a dog sometimes."

"I empathize," said the vet. "No, wait, I sympathize. I always get those two mixed up."

"Really?" I said. The needle loomed closer. "Wh-what's the difference?"

She paused. "Empathy means you know *exactly* what the other person feels because you've gone through the same thing yourself. For instance, I've had mud on my shoes, so I can empathize with what Carolina went through."

She leaned in again with my shot. Yikes! I had to distract her.

"Sympathy is something else?" I asked quickly.

The vet straightened. "Yes. It's sort of the same feeling, but slightly different. You feel sorry for what someone else is going through. But with sympathy, you haven't had the same thing happen to you."

"That is fascinating," I said, hopping off the table. "Well, thanks."

"Anytime, Martha," she replied.

I looked back at Carolina. "Let's go! I'll meet you outside. Hurry!" But when I turned to walk out the door, the vet was blocking it.

"Almost forgot one thing," she said, coming toward me, needle in hand.

The vet drew closer. I squeezed my eyes shut. I felt her hand on my neck. "Okay, doc, I'm ready for my shot."

"That's good, but I just gave it to you," she said.

"You did?" I opened my eyes.
"Hey, that wasn't so bad."

But for the record,
I still do NOT like going
to the vet.

IMPORTANT BUSINESS

On the way home, Carolina tugged at my leash.

"Come on," she said, frowning at the gray sky. "We have to get home. It's going to rain."

"I'm doing important business," I said.

"You're not doing anything. You're just sniffing."

"Don't pressure me," I said. "Empathize a little."

Carolina wrinkled her nose in disgust. "I don't know how you can sniff hydrants. Dogs have the most repellent mannerisms."

"I thought mannerisms were good," I said. "Like saying 'please' and 'thank you.'"

"That's manners," said Carolina. "Mannerisms are things you do a lot. Like if you wave your hands when you talk, or bite your fingernails when you're nervous."

I stopped at a fence. *Sniff!* "Ooo! Rinty was here," I said.

"Hurry up!" begged Carolina. "It's about to rain."

"I told you, I have important business."

"All you have is disgusting dog business," said Carolina. "Eating out of the trash, rolling in mud, sniffing everything."

"That's important," I said.

"Not to me!"

"So?" I replied.

Carolina yanked my leash. "So COME ON!"

I yanked back. "Maybe you should try to have a little sympathy. Maybe you should try walking on a leash! Maybe you should see what it's like to be a dog!"

Suddenly, it began to pour.

"Oh no!" cried Carolina. "I told you!"

We raced home. By the time we burst through the door, we were soaked. I shook myself off.

"Martha!" Carolina shrieked. "You're getting me even wetter!"

"Oops! Sorry," I said.

"I knew this was going to . . to . . . ah-CHOOOO!" Carolina sneezed.

Mom came into the hall. "Oh my!" she said. "Let's get you into some dry clothes and a warm bed."

Carolina followed Mom upstairs.

"Hey, I'm wet and cold too," I called up after them. "Does anybody have sympathy for the dog? Anybody?"

Sigh.

That night, nobody could sleep. In her bed, Helen shifted her swollen ankle and moaned. Across from her, on an inflatable mattress, Carolina sneezed.

"Unggh," moaned Helen.

"Ah-choo!" sneezed Carolina.

"Unggh." "Ah-choo!" "Unggh." "Ah-choo!"

Some sleepover. It was going to be a long night.

THE UNEXPECTED GUEST

The next morning, I was awoken by an unfamiliar bark. I opened one eye and gasped. A collie was lying on Carolina's inflatable mattress!

Ruff-ruff! it barked. (Which in Dog means, "Wow, I feel so much better! Even though I had to sleep on the floor.")

"Um, hello?" I said. "Where did you come from?"

Helen sat up in bed. "Yeah, where *did* that dog come from?"

Ruff? The collie trotted over to the mirror and gaped at her reflection. "OH NO! I'M A DOG!" she howled. She ran in circles, barking like crazy.

That collie is cuckoo, I thought.

"Martha, you'd better get that collie out of here before Carolina sees it," said Helen. "You know she's not a fan of dogs."

Ruff, ruff! barked the collie.

"She says she *is* Carolina." I laughed. "As if."

Ruff! Ruff!

"She says she just woke up as a dog," I told Helen.

I gave the collie a sniff. She didn't smell human. But there was one way to know for

sure. "Let me ask you a question," I said. "Dogs should be on leashes. True or False?"

Ruff!

I gasped. *"True?!* You *are* Carolina!"

For a second opinion, we called Truman, who'd memorized the characteristics of 203 dog breeds, and invited him over. He brought his doctor's kit and T.D., who just had to see Carolina Collie for himself.

"Say aaaah!" said Truman, holding a tongue depressor in front of her.

She opened her mouth. Truman cringed. "Ack! You have bad breath," he said. "But that's characteristic of dogs."

"Characteristic?" I said.

"Characteristics are the things that are special about how you look or act," said Truman. "Carolina has all the characteristics of a dog. She's furry, has four paws and a tail, and barks."

Ruff!

"Carolina says she doesn't want to have the characteristics of a dog," I said. "She wants us to switch her back into a human."

RUFF! RUFF!

"As soon as possible," I added.

Helen hugged her cousin. "Don't worry. We'll get you back to your old self."

"If we can figure out how Carolina became a dog," said Truman, "maybe we can reverse it."

"I've got it!" said T.D. "Maybe she was bitten by some weird half-dog, half-kid creature under a full moon?"

"You're not saying . . ." said Truman.

"Carolina's a WEREDOG!" T.D. exclaimed.

"Hmm. What are the characteristics of a weredog?" asked Truman.

T.D. shrugged. "Like werewolves, I guess. Only doggier."

"Good theory," said Truman, "but there wasn't a full moon last night."

Only Truman would know that, I thought.

T.D. tried again. "Maybe Carolina switched places with a dog. Right now, somewhere out there, there's a dog living in Carolina's body."

"So somewhere the human Carolina is chasing sticks and rolling in mud?" I asked.

Collie Carolina shuddered.

"I'm sure a dog didn't switch places with you," Helen reassured her. "At least, I hope not."

While we were thinking, Carolina began scratching herself.

Truman shone a light into her ears. "It's just what I thought," he said grimly. "I'm afraid there's no easy way to say this."

"What?" asked Helen, alarmed.

"Carolina," Truman announced, "has fleas."

DOG DAZE

"I can empathize," I told Carolina. "Even the best of us get fleas sometimes. But, uh, I'll just stand way over here, okay?" I took a big step back.

Suddenly, Carolina sniffed the air. *Ruff?*

"Mmm. I smell it too," I said. "Come on!"

We ran out the doggie door, following a delicious scent. It led us to the garbage.

"Ooh, look! A burger!" I said. "Dig in!"

Carolina wrinkled her nose. *Ruff!*

"Gross?" I repeated. "You're a dog now. You should learn to cherish these moments when it's just you and the trash."

But Carolina wasn't listening. She was staring at a squirrel. Her legs twitched. But she didn't move.

"Carolina, chasing squirrels is what dogs do," I said. "They're just mannerisms, right? We can't help ourselves. You're a dog now. Trust your instincts."

Trusting *my* instincts, I began eating from the trash.

Too soon, Helen showed up. "Martha!" she cried. "You know you're not supposed to go through the trash."

Next to me, Carolina froze.

"*Carolina?* Bad girl!" Helen scolded. Then she blushed. "I can't believe I'm talking to my cousin like this."

Ruff! Ruff!

"What did she say?" Helen asked.

"She said she's starting to see things from a dog's point of view," I said. "Does that mean she's seeing things from down here?"

Helen shook her head. "A point of view is the way you understand things. When Carolina says she can see things from your point of view, she means she understands them the way you do."

This was true. Because when another squirrel darted by, Carolina didn't hesitate to chase it.

"Carolina!" shouted Helen.

"Heel, girl!" ordered Truman.

"Come back!" called TD.

We all ran after her. But Carolina was faster. She chased the squirrel . . . then a rabbit . . . and then a car. Her *dad's* car.

"Hey, that's my papi," she barked, running after him. "Dad!"

Carolina followed the car all the way to her father's market. When he stepped out, she jumped up to greet him.

Ruff, ruff, ruff, ruff, ruff!

"Ai-yi-yi!" said her dad, pushing her away. "Shoo! Go away, dog!"

"Papi, it's me, Carolina!" she yipped. But he didn't understand Dog.

He hurried into his store. Carolina whimpered outside. She was so upset, she didn't notice Kazuo drive up.

DOGGY EVER AFTER

We were still searching for Carolina when we met her father sweeping in front of his market. We told him that his daughter was now a dog.

"How could that happen?" he asked.

"She was either bitten by a weredog," I said, "or she's just really lucky."

"I don't care if Carolina is a dog," he said. "She's my daughter and I love her. We must find her!"

We all split up to search again. This time, I went to my doggie pals, who were on their way to the hydrant.

"We're looking for Carolina. She's a collie," I told them. "No tags, and— Wait a minute! NO TAGS! I know where she is!"

I raced to the animal shelter. Sure enough, a sad-eyed Carolina lay in a cage beside the front desk. I explained to Kazuo why he had to let her go.

"So you see," I said, "that collie isn't a real dog. She's a person."

"I totally sympathize," said Kazuo. "But if I let every dog that thought it was human out of the shelter, this place would be empty."

"What if I adopt her?" I suggested.

Kazuo shook his head. "That's against section six, rule nineteen of the Dog Shelter

Code: A dog cannot adopt another dog. Even if that dog can speak."

"You just made up that part about speaking, didn't you?" I asked.

"Well, uh . . ."

Before he could answer, Carolina's dad and the kids arrived. "There she is!" he said, rushing to her side. "This dog is my daughter! Release her immediately!"

Kazuo looked at Carolina, and then back at her dad. "Well, she does have your eyes," he admitted.

So we finally got to take her home.

Now Carolina enjoys life as a dog. She plays fetch with her dad, chases squirrels, and splashes in mud puddles. And since dogs don't wear clothes, she doesn't even miss the mall.

Best of all, her dad loves her no matter what. "Even though you're a dog," he says, "I still cherish you."

And they lived happily ever after.

REWIND

Gah. Truman wants me to tell the rest of the story. What's wrong with Carolina being a dog forever? I think that's a dream come true, don't you? But it *was* only a dream. Okay, here's what really happened.

The morning after the sleepover, I woke up to find Carolina crawling to the mirror. She stopped to scratch behind her ear with her toes.

"Uh, hello?" I said.

She looked up. Then she noticed her reflection and smiled. "I'm me!" she exclaimed. "It must have been a dream. What a relief!"

What's a relief? I wondered. *And why is she acting so . . . doggish?*

"Want to go for a walk?" she asked me. "Huh? Huh? Huh?"

"Uh, sure," I answered. "But I don't do leashes."

"Me neither," said Carolina. "No way! I totally understand your point of view."

"Are you *sure* you feel okay?" I asked.

"Yes. And I can empathize with you now."

Helen sat up and stretched. "Who wants breakfast?" she asked.

Skits and I rushed to her side. *Woof, woof, woof!* we barked.

"*Woof*—I mean, me, me, me!" said Carolina, joining us dogs.

I was a little worried that this new Carolina might eat breakfast out of my dog bowl, but she was back to her old self soon enough. *Except* when she sees a squirrel. (Leaping lasagna, can that girl run!)

THE DEAL

Story #2

Make no bones about it, I love being a dog. But as you can see, it's not always a walk in the park. Take what happened to T.D., for example. It all started when Helen and I found him sulking on his front step.

"What's the matter?" she asked.

T.D. sighed. "It's Saturday."

"Isn't that a good thing?" Helen asked.

"No," said TD. "Saturday leads to Sunday, which leads to Monday, and you know what that means."

"Free pineapple topping at Mario's Pizza?" said Helen.

"Nope. School," said T.D. "Let me give you some highlights from this week. Or in my case, *low*lights."

His troubles began on Monday morning when his homework flew out the bus window.

On Tuesday, he'd set his lunch on a bench, where Alvin Merkel accidentally sat on it.

On Wednesday, he got locked in the utility closet. The janitor had to let him out, which Tiffany Blatsky thought was hilarious.

"On Thursday," said T.D., "Alvin Merkel—"

"Sat on your lunch again?" said Helen.

"No," said TD. "He ran into Billy Taber, who sat on my lunch."

"And yesterday?" said Helen.

"The worst day of all!" cried T.D. He told us that during Mrs. Clusky's science class, he'd been drawing instead of paying attention.

"Based on the results of our experiment," she told the class, "we draw a conclusion. The conclusion is what we've found out. What's our conclusion about what happens when you mix baking soda and vinegar? T.D.?"

He looked up from his sketchbook. "Um, toothpaste?"

Mrs. Clusky frowned. "Perhaps you'll be less distracted when you present your own science project on Monday."

T.D. groaned at the memory. "Ugh, school! I wish I never had to go."

I tried to sympathize, but something caught my eye. "SQUIRREL!" I whooped, taking off after it.

"Why couldn't I have been born a dog?" sighed T.D. "Dogs have it easy."

I stopped short. "Did I just hear you say 'Dogs have it *easy*'?"

"No school? No science projects? Compared to people, dogs have it super easy," said T.D.

"Try being me for a day and see how easy it is," I dared him.

"Try being *me* for a day and see how easy it

is," said T.D.

"Deal!"

"Deal!"

We stared each other down, nose to wet nose.

"Wait, what just happened?" asked T.D.

Helen giggled. "You agreed to be Martha for a day and she agreed to be you."

"Great!" said T.D. "I feel better already. Tomorrow, I'm a dog all day long."

"And Monday, I'll be the newest student at Wag-staff City Elementary School," I said.

DOG FOR A DAY

T.D. went home to tell his dad, O.G., about our deal. He'd found him in the garage, working on one of his latest inventions.

"Hmm," said O.G. "So you think it's easier being a dog than a person? I'd say you have an unusual hypothesis."

T.D. looked frightened. *"I do?* Is it contagious?"

O.G. laughed. "No. A hypothesis is a guess or idea about what you think might happen. But to find out if you're right or not, you must conduct an experiment."

"An experiment? Like with microscopes and test tubes?"

"That's one kind of experiment," said O.G. "But an experiment can be any way of testing an idea."

"Or hypothesis," said T.D.

"Exactly! When I was your age, I had

a hypothesis that I could fuel a go-cart on root beer."

"Did it work?" T.D. asked.

"It might have, if I hadn't gotten thirsty," O.G. replied. "The question is, what do you need to change about yourself to become a dog? Let's compare."

"Okay," said T.D., pulling out his sketchbook.

"Dogs are warm-blooded," said O.G.

"I'm warm-blooded," said T.D., drawing himself and a dog.

"They have fur or hair."

"Check," said T.D.

"They chew on bones," added O.G.

"I enjoy a bone."

"Zounds!" said O.G., looking at T.D.'s sketch. "Maybe you're already a dog. Except . . ."

"Except?" said TD.

"Dogs don't draw."

T.D. gulped. "No problem," he said, gently placing the sketchbook on the workbench. "I can go a day without drawing. This is going to be easy."

O.G.'s eyes lit up. "Wait! I have it!"

"Have what?" asked TD.

"A tail."

T.D.'s jaw dropped. "*You* have a tail?"

"No, *you*," said O.G. "To be a dog, you'll need a tail. I'll invent one for you. Don't go anywhere!"

"I'll just be over here, scratching behind my ears with my paw," said T.D. "Ow!"

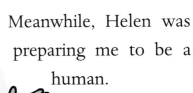

Meanwhile, Helen was preparing me to be a human.

"So let's review what people do and compare that with dogs," she said. "A lot of humans work or, like T.D., they go to school."

I looked up from my bowl. "I was a substitute teacher once."

"Humans eat three meals a day," Helen continued.

"I am eager to try this bonus meal they call lunch," I said.

Just then, a squirrel hopped onto the windowsill. "Uh, excuse me. I have to get this."

WOOF! WOOF! I barked at it.

"*And,*" Helen shouted, "humans don't chase squirrels."

"Right," I said. "Okay. I can go a day without chasing squirrels. Being a human for a day is going to be easy."

NO T.D.s ALLOWED

The next morning, T.D.'s dad was waiting for him in the kitchen.

"Good morning!" said O.G. "Or should I say 'woof-woof'?"

T.D. looked confused.

"Your experiment?" O.G. reminded him. "Dog for a day?"

"Oh, right! I almost forgot," said T.D., dropping to his hands and knees.

"I didn't," I said. T.D. did a double-take. "Just here to observe."

"I'm putting the final touches on your tail," said O.G. He held up a mechanical tail and remote control. "Observe. That means 'watch very closely.'"

He pressed a button and—*whirrrr!* The tail whipped wildly and flew out of his hands.

"Agh!" cried T.D., ducking. The tail skimmed his head and whizzed out of the room.

"Uh, small adjustment necessary," O.G. said. "Anyway, it's time for your breakfast." He set a dog bowl on the floor.

"What's this?" T.D. asked.

"Alphabet soup. Just like Martha eats. It's either that or dog food."

T.D. studied the bowl. "I guess dogs don't use spoons."

"Nope," I said. "Just lean in and lap away."

"Great! Less to clean up," said T.D. He dove in with a loud *slurp!* I have to admit, I was impressed.

"All done!" he said, not bothering to wipe his face. "Now, what should I do today? Oh, that's right. I'm a dog, which means I can do . . . whatever I want!"

T.D. was a natural. He played fetch. He rolled in the grass. He even chewed a rubber bone—and *liked* it.

"I love being a dog!" he said. "What else do dogs do all day?"

"Root through the trash behind the grocery store?" I suggested.

"Maybe later. What else?" T.D. asked.

"Run after passing cars?"

"Sounds dangerous," he said. "I know! I'll go see if some of my friends can play. That's something dogs do."

First we went to my house. But Helen was busy cleaning her room. Then we visited Truman. But he was helping his dad take newspapers to the recycling center.

"New hypothesis," said T.D. as we headed home. "Humans devote too much time to chores."

"Ready to give up?" I asked.

"No way," said T.D. "It proves my point. People have it harder than dogs."

The darkening sky rumbled. "Uh-oh. Looks like rain," I said.

"No problem," said T.D. "I'll hang out at the library."

"Don't think so," I said. "Dogs don't have library cards. And . . . well, you'll see."

At the library, T.D. stared at the sign on the front door.

"No dogs allowed?" he said. "That doesn't seem fair."

"Now that you're a dog, T.D., you're going to discover the one thing every canine knows: it's a human world we live in."

With that, it began to pour.

"Human or canine," said T.D., "we have to get out of the rain. And we're pretty far from home."

"Looks like I'll have to teach a new dog old tricks," I said. We waited out the storm underneath the porch of a nearby house. After a while, T.D.'s stomach growled.

"Hope it stops soon," said T.D. "It's almost lunchtime."

"Hate to be the one to break it to you, but dogs don't eat lunch. Unless you happen to sniff out something yummy in a trash can," I said.

"Ew," said T.D.

"Ready to admit that it's harder being a dog?" I asked.

T.D. chased his imaginary tail before settling down again. "Just wait till you have to be a human tomorrow and go to school," he said. "I think you'll come to a very different conclusion."

DOGS DON'T DRAW

Back at T.D.'s house, we shook off the rain.

"Now I'm really hungry," he said, reaching for the refrigerator.

"Not so fast," I warned. "You do know dogs can't open refrigerator doors, right?"

"Uh, right," said TD. "No problem."

"If you bark, someone may eventually get annoyed enough to feed you."

"HUNGRY!" he hollered at once. "VERY HUNGRY!"

O.G. appeared in the doorway with a new mechanical tail. "T.D.! Just the dog I was looking for," he said. "It's time for your dinner."

O.G. placed a bowl on the floor.

"Soup again?" moaned T.D.

"Dogs don't have much variety in their meals," I explained.

"Soup it is," said T.D. He planted his face in the bowl.

About this time, Helen arrived. She giggled at the sight of T.D. "How's the great dog-for-a-day experiment going?" she asked.

"Kind of messy," said T.D. "But it's a lot easier than being in school."

O.G. attached the mechanical tail to the back of T.D.'s pants. "Finished!" he said. "Observe."

He clicked the remote control. The tail began to twirl, faster and faster. Suddenly, it lifted into the air, nearly taking T.D.'s pants with it. *Snap!* went his waistband.

"Owwww!" howled T.D.

The tail flew out the kitchen window. We watched O.G. chase it around the yard.

"Now that's something you don't see every day," I said. "A human chasing his tail."

Helen decided that was her cue to go. After she left, T.D. reached for his sketchbook on the coffee table.

"Uh-uh," I said.

"What?" he asked.

"I thought maybe you were about to draw."

"No way!" T.D. protested. "Everyone knows dogs don't draw. I'll just be over here scratching behind my ears."

He plopped down, repeating to himself, "Dogs don't draw. Dogs don't draw. Dogs don't draw."

That night, curled up in a dog bed, he was still murmuring it in his sleep.

SO YOU STILL WANT TO BE A DOG?

The next morning, Helen found T.D. sketching in the schoolyard.

"You really missed drawing, didn't you?" she asked.

"A little bit," he said. "Where's Martha?"

Helen shrugged. "She wasn't at breakfast."

"Aha!" said T.D., smiling. "She's only been a human for an hour and she's already late. Not like being a dog, where you don't have to be anywhere on time."

But when they walked into homeroom, they were in for a surprise.

"Hi, guys!" I said.

"Martha! You're here," said Helen.

Yup. Not only was I at school, but it turns out I'm pretty good at it. I didn't even eat my homework. Helen was proud. T.D. wasn't as pleased.

After class, he grumbled, "Martha knew the capital of South Dakota. How did she do that?"

"Martha's smart," said Helen.

"Maybe my hypothesis was wrong," said T.D. "It's a lot easier for Martha to be a human than it was for me to be a dog."

"Don't jump to any conclusions," said Helen. "The experiment isn't over yet."

"Maybe not. But I can already see the results," he said.

T.D. joined me outside for lunch. I was enjoying the contents of my own paper bag.

"Mmm!" I said, licking my chops. "People have come up with some great inventions. But the best one ever is lunch."

T.D. took a bite out of his sandwich and sighed. "The results are not good," he said.

"That's okay. I'll eat them," I offered.

"Results aren't food," said T.D. "A result is what happens when you do something."

"Oh, like as a result of eating lunch, I'm happy?" I asked.

"Yes. And the results of this experiment show that you were right about being a dog," he said. "It is easier to be a person than to be a dog. I was a very bad dog." He scolded himself: "Bad dog!"

"You're not a bad dog," I said, jumping up beside him. "Can I tell you a secret? Being a human hasn't been easy at all."

"It hasn't?" asked T.D.

"No, it was hard," I confessed. "I had to memorize all those state capitals, get up early, and you're not even allowed to fall asleep in class."

"Tell me about it," said T.D.

"I'd say your experiment has taught us a lot."

"Experiment!" he cried. "Oh no! I'm supposed to present a science project this afternoon!"

"Didn't we just *live* a pretty good science experiment?" I asked.

"You're right!" T.D. exclaimed. He grabbed his sketchbook and wrote:

Hypothesis: It's easier being a dog than a person.

Later that day, he presented his science project to the class.

"So the conclusion of my experiment is that it's just as hard to be dog as it is to be a person. But either way," T.D. said, smiling at Helen and me, "it's easier if you have friends."

Woof! I barked in agreement. Having human *and* canine friends made me one lucky dog!

From then on, T.D. and Carolina never thought dogs had it easy again. But hey, you don't have to take their word for it. You can try being a dog for a day too. Maybe even . . . today!

(Just remember, no eating your homework!)

GLOSSARY

How many words do you remember from the story?

characteristic: something that is special about how you look or act.

conclusion: what you've found out from an experiment.

empathy: knowing what another person feels because you've gone through the same thing yourself.

experiment: any way of testing an idea.

hypothesis: a guess or idea about what you think might happen.

mannerism: a gesture or action you do a lot.

observe: to watch very closely.

point of view: the way you understand things.

result: what happens when you do something.

sympathy: feeling sorry for what someone else is going through even though you haven't had the same thing happen to you.

MARTHA'S DOG-FOR-A-DAY
EXPERIMENT

Ever wonder what life is like from a pooch's point of view? Then conduct your own dog-for-a-day experiment!

Here's what to do:

Step 1

Observe the behavior of humans and dogs. Compare their characteristics and mannerisms in a notebook, just like T.D. did.

Step 2

Next, write down your hypothesis. If you need help, simply fill in the blank: Dogs are more _____ than humans.

Step 3

Pick a day to be a dog. (Martha suggests a weekend. Dogs don't go to school!) Tell your family and friends so they can play along.

Step 4

On the day of your experiment, act like a dog from morning to bedtime.

Step 5

When you're done, record the results and your conclusion. Were they what you expected? What kind of dog were you? Draw a picture!

PICK-ME-UP
POOCH

If you feel sympathy or empathy for someone, show them you care with a dog card.

1 Fold a square piece of paper in half to make a triangle.

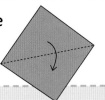

2 Fold two corners of the triangle down to make ears.

3 Draw some eyes, a nose, and a mouth. Write your message on the back or under one of the ears!